I0631145

Gertrude Smith

Practical programs for school and home entertainments

With supplement of ten dialogues in rhyme for little folks

Gertrude Smith

Practical programs for school and home entertainments
With supplement of ten dialogues in rhyme for little folks

ISBN/EAN: 9783337273910

Printed in Europe, USA, Canada, Australia, Japan

Cover: Foto ©Andreas Hilbeck / pixelio.de

More available books at **www.hansebooks.com**

PRACTICAL PROGRAMS

FOR

School and Home Entertainments.

A SERIES OF EXERCISES INTRODUCING NOVEL AND
ATTRACTIVE FEATURES

BY

MAUDE M. JACKSON.

WITH SUPPLEMENT OF
TEN DIALOGUES IN RHYME FOR LITTLE FOLKS.

CHICAGO:
A. FLANAGAN, PUBLISHER.

CONTENTS:

Busy Boys of Uncle Sam - - - - -	40
Carnival of Muses - - - - -	64
Christmas Chimes - - - - - -	15
Decoration Day - - - - - -	56
Dewey Day Program - - - - -	34
Kite Drill - - - - - - -	38
Little Sweepers - - - - - -	47
Literary Re-Union - - - - -	7
Mother Goose Boys - - - - - -	42
Memorial Day - - - - - -	53
Our Nation's Pride - - - - - -	50
Pantomime - - - - - - -	84
Patriotic Program - - - - -	59
Queen of the Year - - - - - -	76
Rolling Pin Drill - - - - - -	45
Ten Dialogues in Rhyme - - - -	87
Washington's Birthday - - - - -	29
Young America's Patriotism - - - -	31

PREFACE.

In presenting this series of exercises to the progressive teachers, the author knows from practical presentation of the work in a large number of the Chicago schools that the book supplies a long felt want in this line. For the past four years these exercises have been developed under the author's personal direction and have proven eminently successful.

The secret of success in preparing programs lies in presenting the work in the happiest and most enthusiastic manner at the *very first drill*. Select the characters to be used, and before any parts are given out *go over the whole drill, or drama*, or whatever may be the exercise, in an earnest and effective manner, so that each child may see in what spirit his part may be developed and understand *his part* in *relation* to the *whole*.

It has been the author's desire to encourage the spirit of natural enjoyment pupils should feel in developing an entertainment, hence the work is largely free from set mechanical drill and military precision, which is exhausting to both pupil and teacher. The object of the text has been to aid the natural ease and gracefulness which all children possess, if they are given interesting and congenial methods by which to express themselves.

MAUDE M. JACKSON.

LITERARY REUNION.

A literary sketch introducing American classics in impersonation. Plan, Washington Irving holds a reception and the following celebrated authors appear giving comment upon their own most famous work.

Stage arranged in easy manner of reception room. Let the "authors" be familiar with the character of the writer they represent, thus correlating their work in literature with their program. If possible have hung about the stage pictures of the authors represented. Time about twenty minutes.

CHARACTERS.

WASHINGTON IRVING.	HARRIET BEECHER STOWE.
BENJ. FRANKLIN.	HELEN HUNT JACKSON.
NATHANIEL HAWTHORNE.	JULIA WARD HOWE.
H. W. LONGFELLOW.	ALICE CARY.
JAMES RUSSELL LOWELL.	PHOEBE CARY.
OLIVER WENDELL HOLMES.	LOUISA ALCOTT.

Costume if desired.

Scene. Reception room. Washington Irving pacing back and forth as he speaks.

Irving. And so I have bidden to-day to meet those delightful men and women who have followed me in the pleasing path of letters. Little did I think, when I penned the Whim Whams of Launcelot Lanstaff and wrote the Knickerbocker History of New York, and then happily run on into my Sketch Book, which was so cordially received in both Europe and America, and brought me the pleasing title of "First ambassador of letters the New World sent to the Old." Little, I repeat, did I think that after over one hundred years my name should be so generally and heartily loved. The Legends of Sleepy Hollow, with quaint old Rip Van Winkle and the description of Icabod Crane still amuse and entertain my kind friends. (Enter Benj. Franklin, Hawthorne and Longfellow.) To meet Benj. Franklin, the philospher and statesman to whom the American people owe so much gratitude is indeed an esteemed privilege. (Shakes hands with Franklin.) And these two younger lights, close friends and school companions, Henry Wadsworth Longfellow and Nathaniel Hawthorne is a great pleasure. I greet you most cordially.

Franklin. Respected friends, I am glad to be among you. In all my foresight for my beloved country I could not foretell in what manner her noble sons would distinguish themselves. In my missions to foreign lands I could not but feel amid the glow and glitter and pomp of European circles that the sturdy simplicity of our young nation would be a tower of strength in forming the country's welfare. I am proud to know how the skill and genius of America's sons have advanced the education of the world.

Hawthorne. Honored sir, we feel in the presence of your towering intelligence like the passing song birds of summer resting in the shadow and strength of a majestic evergreen whose freshness and vigor rejoice the heart.

Longfellow. Nobly said, friend Nathaniel. To the masterful mind of this pioneer of thought and action, the science of to-day owes its early impetus. From the simple experiment of the now famous kite, we have to-day flashing around the world, light, intelligence and motion, and the whole range of affairs, social, commercial and scientific, have changed.

Hawthorne. And to the youth of America remains that model of philosophical thought, Franklin's Antibiography. (Voices outside.)

Franklin. You are kind. More friends are with us. (Enter Holmes, Lowell, Harriet B. Stowe, Mrs. Howe. General greeting.)

Irving. I bid you welcome. No introductions are necessary here.

Holmes. Indeed no! We have been laid together upon the same shelf for too many years not to be able to recognize each other now. To these ladies we extend our kindest greeting and most sincere admiration.

Mrs. Stowe. Dr. Holmes, you are most gallant and we are most grateful. (To Franklin and Irving.) Worthy sirs, to you our greatest re spects.

Lowell. A most delightful meeting. To be among these distinguished men and women is an honor I greatly appreciate.

Mrs. Howe. It is rare indeed to find myself in such congenial company. Living as I have in these changeful times, I can see what a powerful influence these men of thought have had, and are having upon the youth of to-day. Washington Irving, Franklin, are names that command world wide homage. Nathaniel Hawthorne, you hold a place unique in American literature. To you, dear Longfellow, the smallest child as well as the mature man and woman can turn with love. Your words have become household possessions. Evangeline with whom we have all wept; Hiawatha and the wonderful tradititions, we love them all. Even your smaller gems find a resting place in every human heart. Let us hear from your own lips the final sentiment of the Launching of the Ship.

Longfellow. You are very flattering. My heart thrilled with the deepest patriotism as I penned these words. (Repeat from Launching of the Ship, beginning: Thou too sail on, etc. All applaud.)

Lowell. Let us be favored with some thought from each of the guests present.

Irving. A charming suggestion. (Enter rest of cast.)

Holmes. (Advancing to meet them.) Ah! Here are our younger friends. We welcome you. Unfortunately you are too late to hear what your honored friend has said to us. (General greeting. Boys place chairs for ladies.)

Louisa Alcott. But not too late, I trust, to hear from you.

Mrs. Stowe. (Advancing and greeting each.) Louisa, Phoebe and Alice, my heartiest welcome to you. These two sisters whose tender pretty gems (placing arms about Phoebe and Alice) breathe of their happy home, are very dear to the American people.

Phoebe. That we were accorded a place, even away back in the tiniest corner of this talented gathering, is I think a surprise to both of us. We sang for love, not fame, and our thoughts came with the flowers of spring and the clouds of summer.

Alice. We are indeed grateful. I am told that this little effort of mine is often praised. (Repeat, The Burning Prairie, found in No. 2 Standard Selections.)

Mrs. Stowe. (Leans over Louisa's chair as address is given.) Louisa, you are the idol of the youth of America. Your dear Little Women are ours, Meg, Beth and Joe, we love them all.

Louisa. Do you know, kind friends, Joe's

experience in preparing her first story was really my own. I hold the affection of the children as the dearest result of my long labors. I have received hundreds of letters from kind admiring friends.

Lowell. Helen Hunt, your noble championship of the cause of the Red Man awakened a much needed interest in the original American.

Helen Hunt. I felt the cause I championed most deeply and am glad to know that through the agency of my books, A Century of Dishonor, Ramona, and my versified thoughts, I helped to arouse a more kindly interest in the cause of this unhappy people. As wards of a great nation, *justice should* guide its dealings with them.

Hawthorne. Will you not give to us one or two lines from that beautiful poem of yours, "Not as I will"?

Helen Hunt. With pleasure. (Recite final stanzas of poem "Not as I will.")

Mrs. Howe. Dr. Holmes, we have not heard from you. The Autocrat and Poet ought not to lose an opportunity to add a thought of his own.

Dr. Holmes. The ladies first! Mrs. Stowe, you have not given us your contribution. We know, of course, of your famous Uncle Tom's Cabin, how and where it was written and what a wonderful effect it had upon the question of the day. But of your other thoughts; tell us of them.

Mrs. Stowe. Like Topsey, "Dey jist growed."

Dr. Holmes. James Russell Lowell, the author of the Bigelow papers, should be in strong sympathy with the creator of Uncle Tom's Cabin, as similar convictions make them allies.

Lowell. Yes, my sentiments in regard to the times still are expressed in the words of "The Crisis."

> "Once to every man and nation
>   Comes the moment to decide,
> In the strife with truth and falsehood
>   For the good or evil side.
> Some great cause, God's great Messiah
>   Offering each the bloom or blight,
> Parts the goats upon the left hand
>   And the sheep upon the right,
> And the choice goes by forever
>   Twixt that darkness and the light."

(All applaud.)

Dr. Holmes. Those sentiments are most lofty. Mrs. Howe, all have given their gems but you.

Mrs. Howe. You forget *yourself*, Dr. Holmes!

Dr. Holmes. You do not wish me to give them all together and no part first, like the finale of the "One Hoss Shay?"

Mrs. Howe. I will tell you, friends, how the words of this Battle Hymn of the Republic came to be written. During the early part of the

Civil War, myself and a party of friends were riding on the outskirts of the city, when we were suddenly surrounded by the advance guard of the rebel army. The ladies for a moment were frightened, but we were finally permitted to return. Then the ladies sang "John Brown's Body" in defiant tones. I said then that so grand an air should have better words, and in the grey of the following dawn the words sang themselves through my mind and I rose, and not seeing the lines wrote them down. I am glad they have lived.

Irving. As a compliment to their talented author and a tribute to our native land before we part let us join in singing the hymn.

(Group together Irving and Franklin, Mrs. Stowe, Dr. Holmes, Mrs. Howe, Lowell, Alice Carey, Longfellow, Phoebe Carey, Hawthorne, Louisa Alcott, Helen Hunt. Sing three stanzas of Battle Hymn. Let the conversation be easy and natural. Move about as in a parlor. *Let each actor study well the character of the author.* I repeat this suggestion because of its importance.)

CHRISTMAS CHIMES CANTATA

OR

SANTA CLAUS' DILEMMA.

ACT I.

SCENE 1. Santa Claus' Workshop. "What shall I do?" "Send for the Fairies!"

SCENE 2. Arrival of Fairies. Santa's Dilemma. The Solution. Fairies go on a good mission.

ACT II.

SCENE 1. Mother Goose's Home. Arrival of Fairies. Mother Goose consents.

SCENE 2. Fairy Leaders call their Bands and tell them of Invitation. All are delighted.

ACT III.

SCENE 1. Return from the Wedding. Mother Goose's Children welcome Santa Claus. All promise to assist. The Merrymaking. Departure to work for Christmas.

SCENE 2. Margery's Dream, and its Realization.

Final Tableaux. (All grades included.)

CAST OF CHARACTERS.

Santa Claus
Mother Goose
Snow Queen
King Winter
Queen Titania
Prince of the Brownies
King of Elves
Floppity-fly (Santa's servant)
Jack Horner
Cinderella
Boy Blue
Old Mother Hubbard
Red Riding Hood
Beauty
{ Bachelor
{ Wife
Maiden All Forlorn

Bo Peep
Woman who rode White Horse
Queen's Page
Jack Be Nimble
Scheherezade
Mistress Mary
Miss Moffett
Flower Queen
Dreamer
15 Greenwood Fairies
15 Snow Fairies
15 Elves
15 Brownies
6 Flowers, Chrysanthemums
8 Little Jacks
Postman
20 Sailors

15

(A smaller number of children may be used.)
Time, two hours.

Costumes—Greenwood fairies in green of thin material. Snow fairies in white. Elves tight-fitting green suits. Chrysanthemums, yellow and white crepe paper. Other costumes to suit characters.

Anyone wishing further instuction address, with enclosed stamp,   MAUDE M. JACKSON,
                          256 Humboldt Boul., Chicago.

Act I. Scene 1. Santa's work shop—bench, tools, broken toys, pack, etc., letters.

Santa seated at table reading letters.—Long list on roller.

S. C. Two weeks until Christmas time, and my work no where near finished. Look at this monstrous list of addresses, and at this huge pile of letters, and every day brings more. How ever I am to get through with this big contract, I can't see. I am fairly swamped in the rush of orders. (Rings bell, enter servant). Floppity fly, bring in my tools, I must not lose a minute now. Where is my apron? (Enter Flop, with tools). (Postman's whistle out side). Another load of orders I suppose. (Enter postman with big sack of letters, Santa throws up hands in despair). Floppity fly! What on earth am I to do. Most of them rush orders too.

Flop. If you will allow me, my merry Santa Claus, let me suggest you send for your good friends the fairies to help you out. They dearly love the children.

S. C. Capital! You are a genius, Floppity fly; go and telephone for King Winter, Queen Snow, Queen Titania, King of the Elves, and Prince of the Brownies. Here are the telephone numbers, (Reads as Flop writes them down) King Winter, No. 40 below zero, North Pole. Queen Titania, No. 99 Woodland Glen. King of Elves, No. 602, Idlewild Forest. Prince of Brownies, No. 702, Greenwood Cave. Call them up and tell them to meet here tonight for an important convention. Be sure you get them to answer, and don't let any one switch you off the line until you get word to them.

Flop. At once, good Santa Claus. Here are your tools on the bench. (Flop rings up Winter).

Hello! Hello! Is this King Winter? Hold the line. Are you there? Santa Claus. Yes, Santa Claus wants you to come to his workshop at 8 sharp tonight, to attend an important convention. No. Yes. All right, Goodbye.

Hello! Hello! Is this Queen Titania? Santa Claus presents his compliments and earnestly desires you to attend an important convention at his work shop to-night. You will be there with pleasure? All right, goodbye.

Hello! Hello! Is this 602 Idlewild Forest? Santa Claus sends his regards and desires you to come to his work shop to-night at 8—Yes. All of them. What? Oh! The Prince of the Brownies is there with you, (turns to S. C.) Santa Claus, the Prince is with the King of the Elves, Shall I tell him now to come?

S. C. I'll speak to him. Hello Prince, where did you come from? What, you've been over to Manila and down to Cuba, good! Be sure to be here at 8 sharp. There's a big business meeting here—Goodbye, I must be at work every second.

Now Floppity fly, I shall have to go over to Norway for an hour or two, to order the Christmas trees. I'll be back in time to get ready for the fairies. (Exit S. C).

Flop arranges room for guests. (Sings).

"Christmas is coming so merry and gay,
 Nature is mantled in white,
Children are eagerly waiting the day,
 Singing from morning till night." (Exit.)

Scene 2. Enter Santa Claus. Begins work, pounding to time of lively galop. Sings—(Air, Mikado, "I've Got 'em on the List.")

You may talk about your busy men,
 With brain, or pen, or fist,
 I've got a little list; I've got a little list,
Of children who are good or bad,
 And no one shall be missed,
 For I've got 'em on the list. I've got 'em on the list.

Here's the little boy who wants a top;
  And skates and marbles too—
Here's the little girl who wants a doll,
  All dressed in bright sky blue,
And the baby boy who wants a top
  Are all down on the list,
  And no one shall be missed.   No one shall be missed.

Music, galop. Enter Winter, Snow, Titania, King and Prince.
Dance down centre to front.

S. C. I knew you would be on time. Queen Snow, I salute you. Queen Titania, your beauty grows with the years. King Winter, you and I have been partners for so many years we are quite familiar friends. King of the Elves, I welcome you; you and you, dear Prince, are a very dear friend to my beloved children. And now there is not a moment to waste. I must tell you why I called you in. I am in a great *dilemma!* Look here! (Points to big pile of letters and list.) All this to be attended to in three weeks and my work not half done. I must have help, and I knew your love for the children would lead you to offer some advice and assistance.

Queen Snow. Now, Santa Claus, I have told you before you ought to get married. King Winter would not be able to get through half his work without me.

S. C. But my dear friends! You don't comprehend! You cannot realize how hard it would be to find a wife for a man who has the cares and responsibilities that I carry. What woman could be found who would be willing to join fortunes with a party who has a list of children like this to provide for. It would be no use spending valuable time looking for such an impossible character. Only a woman who has similar cares can appreciate me.

(Fairies consult on side. Together exclaim) We have it! Mother Goose!

S. C. (Sits down in amazement.) Bless me! I never thought of her. But she is a good soul, and I admire her greatly. But do you really think she is "goose" enough to join fortunes with me?

Titania. Well, Santa Claus, we cannot promise you success; but I think it likely, as she is so attached to the children the world over.

Elf King. Yes, Santa Claus, go and ask her. You certainly need help right here all the time, because it would never do to be behind-hand with your Christmas things.

Prince of Brownies. We all pledge you to do all we can to help you along. (Together they sing with pretty swing movement. Air Pinafore: Buttercup.)

> Oh! yes! We'll help Santa Claus,
> Darling Old Santa Claus,
>   Working so hard night and day,
> We'll join in the working, not one of us shirking,
>   And make Christmas merry and gay.—(*Repeat.*)

King Winter. Now Santa, lose no time. Go to Mother Goose and get the matter settled. (Santa, assisted by Flop, makes toilet. Winter, King and Prince group back. Snow and Titania sing. Air, Mikado, "Punishment fit the Crime.")

To Mother Goose we'll go, as light as winds that blow,
And let her know that Santa Claus
Is coming onward to propose. (*Exit Santa*)
He need not know we're there,
But her we will prepare,
And make the meeting glad and gay,
To help the merry Christmas day. (*Exit all.*)

Act II. Scene I. Home of Mother Goose. Mother Goose sweeping down to the stage centre front.

Well! Well! Nearly Christmas time again and all the boys need new suits. Boy Blue has completely spoiled his jacket and Tommy Tucker looks like a fright. Dear, dear; its pretty hard to be all alone to look after this big family. (Music.) Law me! Some one must be coming. (Enter Queens with short pretty dance. Mother Goose curtesies.)

M. G. Welcome! Most welcome, Royal ladies. I am honored by your visit.

Q. Titania. We can stay but a moment. We came to give you warning.

M. G. (in surprise.) A warning!

Snow Queen. Yes! Santa Claus is on his way here to propose to you! He feels lonely and needs a good, sensible wife to help him with his many cares. We happened to find out his intentions and came to give you notice. He will be here shortly. Receive him kindly. Don't let him know we came.

Queen T. You both so dearly love the children I am sure you will be happy together. We give you our blessing in advance. We must go. (Music for dance. Exit.)

M. G. Well, did you ever! I am so flustered! Where is my clean apron? I am glad all the boys are away. Hark! Hear those sleigh bells! Here he comes!

S. C. (outside.) Whoa, Dancer! Whoa, Prancer! Whoa, Dunder and Blitzen! (Enter S. C.)

M. G. I am very much surprised, but very glad to see you, Santa.

S. C. I am also much surprised, and am very glad to find you at home! I am a very busy man, Mother Goose, and, and--ahem!--

M. G. Having so many children of my own I can understand.

S. C. So you can! So you can! Now, did you ever think you would like--hem! Dear me! How warm it is in here!

Mother G. Do you find it so? Shall I call in the boys to open the windows?

S. C. No! No! Not just now, as I am in a hurry!—A great hurry! I came to—to—

M. G. Yes?

S. C. I came to see if you would like to get married?

M. G. Dear me! You quite astonish me, Santa Claus! To whom should I be married?

S. C. To me! We are both happy, busy people. We can help each other and make the children all over the world so happy.

M. G. Well! I am a sensible woman. Yes, I think it might be a wise plan, and we can arrange for Christmas together.

S. C. Dear Mother Goose! You *are* a good, kind soul and will make the children happy. I will come for you tomorrow. Good-bye. Invite everybody—

M. G. Good-bye, Santa Claus. You will have to hurry, and so will I. I shall be ready. Good-bye—Good-bye! (Exit S. C.) Now I must tell the children. We must invite Cinderella and the Prince, Red Riding Hood and all the fairies and elves, and have a merry wedding. My! But I must hurry. (Exit.)

Scene II. Pantomime Fairy Scene—Stage Clear—Good Waltz —Enter at opposite sides, Queen Titania, Queen Snow—Waltz together.

Queen Snow chimes bells, enter 15 fairies, circle in ring. Queen Titania waves wand, enter 15 green fairies, circle in ring, all kneel, Queens circle and tell each. All clap hands, rise; Queens meet at back, forward by twos, one white, one green; divide at stage center; Queens to the center, back; arrange long line at back, in couples, waltz. Enter opposite wings, King of Elves, Prince of Brownies; meet at stage center (Fairies at back); leaders dance; separate; King of Elves blows horn, enter Green Elves—bells on toes, cloth slippers in point. Prince claps hands, enter Brownies; circle same as above. Form in two lines across stage, one line Fairies one line Brownies and Elves; face; Fairies and Elves join right hands, Fairies and Brownies same; circle around, face left, all join hands; Fairy leaders dance to end of line; all follow in circle round stage, twice. Exit.

Act III. Scene I. Mother Goose's home; return from wedding; enter Flop, sings (air, ''Five and Twenty Blackbirds''):

Mother Goose is married, they're all coming now,
Get ready, all ye little folks, to make your nicest bow;
(Enter S. C. and M. G.) Santa Claus and Mother Goose,
Oh! Happy may you be, and we all will dance
So gaily, round the merry Xmas tree—

(Enter bridal party, leaders of Fairies), two seats at stage center for S. C. and M. G. high.

S. C. (rising.) My dear, kind friends, your cordial good wishes are very pleasant. Mother Goose, call in your little folks and let me greet them.

M. G. Every one of the dear little folks have pledged themselves to assist good Santa Claus in his big Christmas enterprise, and I know you will love them all. (Calls) Boy Blue! (Enter B. B.) Yes, mother! (Kneels.)

M. G. Santa Claus wants to see all of the children who are at home. Run and blow your horn for them. (Blows horn.) (Lively gallop.) (Enter all Mother Goose's children, form circle, kneel, rise, pass to place after Santa's welcome.)

S. C. Welcome, my pretty dears. There, now, my little man, lift out your pretty wife and use your wheel-barrow to help me deliver my Christmas goods, because my reindeer team is not equal to the whole task. Why, I used to do the United States in two or three hours, but now I have to circle the whole world to reach all the bright little folks who rejoice under the Stars and Stripes.

M. G. Come here, children. Mistress Mary, quite contrary. Santa Claus, I can hardly do anything with her. She means well, but she has *such* a temper! Poor Beauty, here, has a hard time with her. Beauty, go and get Scheherezade of the Arabian Nights. I want her to tell a Christmas story. (Exit.) You Maiden all forlorn, go and see if the marines are ready to help Santa Claus about those island contracts. (Exit.)

Prince of Brownies. If they come, Mother Goose, we fairy folks will run away and get our little bands ready also. Will you excuse us, Santa Claus?

S. C. Surely.

M.G. Children, run away now for a little while, we wish to see the marines alone. (Exit. Enter sailors; good lively music; marines carry long rope. Salute, drill.)

S. C. I am very glad of your service. Go to my work shop. I will greet you there shortly. (Exit. Enter children.)

M. G. Come here, children. Jack Hormer, Santa, begins to think he is too old to do the Christmas pie act and he has been teaching some of the other little fellows how to do this part of the performance. (Jack whistles, enter 8 little Jacks with pies.)

M. G. Girls, sing for the boys. (All sing the "Baby" song from Wang. Boys act in pantomime.)

M. G. Sing for Miss Moffett. (All sing as before.) Sing for Bo Peep. (All sing as before.) Sing for Mother Hubbard. (Words.)

> "Old Mother Hubbard she went to the cupboard
>   To get her poor dog a bone,
> And when she got there the cupboard was bare
>   And so the poor doggie had none."

M. G. You remember, Santa Claus, that the woman who rode on the white horse with rings on her fingers and bells on her toes really meant Queen Elizabeth. Run and get her, Red Riding Hood. (Enter Beauty.)

Beauty. Here is Scheherezade, Mother. (Low salute.)

M. G. After Queen Elizabeth arrives, we will hear your story.

King Winter. Send for our little ones and let us see how light their feet are. (Exit Fairy leaders.)

S. C. Now for the story. (Sche. recite any good Xmas piece. Music. Enter all fairies.)

Queen T. (To one of her band.) Greenleaf, run and see if the flowers are ready for Santa Claus.

Snow Queen. (To one of her band.) Snow-flake, show us how the snow comes down! (Pretty dance. Enter flowers. Flower Queen, sing air from Mikado, air, Titwillow. Flowers act in pantomime.) Sings.

Oh! We are the flowers of gay Christmas time
   And we're nodding, we're nodding, we're nodding,
And we come with our curly locks loose in the wind
   As we're nodding and nodding and nodding,
We love merry Christmas and dear Santa Claus,
   And we know that he loves us and that is because
When he sees our bright faces he always will pause,
   As we're nodding and nodding and nodding.

Oh! We are Chrysanthemums, as you may see
   As we're nodding and nodding and nodding,
And we come with the snow-flakes so happy and free
   As we're nodding, and nodding and nodding,

> We are off to the wedding of dear Mother Goose,
> And as gay little flowers may all be of use,
> We will shake out our petals so fluffy and loose
> As we're nodding and nodding and nodding.

Elf King. Kickety Go, sing about Christmas. (Any Christmas song here.)

Prince of Brownies. Bibbity Bobble, sing about the Brownies. (Song.)

S. C. And now, kind friends, no one can enjoy this happy merry making more than I do, but time presses. Mother Goose and I have so much to do, we will have to get right at work. As you all have agreed to help, I have written down my directions here and will hand each one a list of the duties he is to perform. All sing. (Airs, Buttercup; Yes, we'll help Santa Claus, Darling old Santa Claus, etc. Santa Claus names *all* leading characters and hands each envelope.)

King of Elves. I see you have given us directions to use our little bands as they feel they will do the most good. (Fairies kneel about their leaders. All cry, " Now Away." General exit.)

Scene III. Small child in bed, hears bells.

Margery. I wonder if the fairies do come with Santa Claus every Christmas Eve? I am going to hang up my stocking and then get into bed and just stay awake and watch for them. (Bells outside. Runs to window.) No, they are not there. (Gets into bed and falls asleep. Enter fairies with Christmas tree; enter Santa; fills stockings. All characters quietly take place on stage. Child wakes; Margarey grasps stocking and cries, "Oh! here they all are. I must run and tell mama!" Exit.)

CHORUS—Merry Christmas to all, and to all good night.

Good march. (Exit.)

AN EXERCISE FOR WASHINGTON'S BIRTHDAY.

Short Historical Sketch for Second and Third Grades.

SING—(Air, "Marching thro' Georgia.")

> Today we tell the story, each year the tale renew,
> Of Washington, so noble, of his courage tried and true;
> He gave to us a nation, for his valor, force and zeal,
> Inspired the land to conflict and made the tyrant kneel.

1—W   While a child his truth and courage
          We all can plainly see,
        When we learn about the story
          Of the hatchet and the tree.

2—A   As a youth, so strong and fearless,
          He swam thro' waters wild,
        Which raged and roared about him
          To save a little child.

3—S   Swiftly onward thro' the forest
          And country bleak and cold,
        Four hundred miles he traveled
          When but twenty-one years old.

4—H His steady skill and wisdom,
His earnestness and truth,
Made him respected, honored,
When he was but a youth.

5—I In each and every dnty
He fulfilled so steadfastly,
We can find a good example
To follow every day.

6—N Now we revere his memory
On this day in all our land,
We remember all the struggles
Of the feeble patriot band.

7—G Get ready, then, your banners,
Let the Stars and Stripes wave high,
In honor to the name of one
Whose fame will never die.

8—T Together we will praise him
In our songs of earnest cheer,
Remembering we owe to him
Our country grand and dear.

9—O O'er all our rich, broad country
Today the children sing
Of his noble deeds and daring,
To the breeze the flag they fling.

10—N Now, join we all together,
Read his name in letters bold,
Sing with us now the anthem
That never shall grow old.

SING—"My Country, 'tis of thee."

SUGGESTIONS.—A picture of Washington, on an easel, can be used, and one girl, as Columbia, may place a wreath of evergreens around the picture. All girls with flags raise them toward picture, with letter held on the breast, if letters are used, and pose for a tableaux. These letters can be the "busy" work for the children, who thus make them for this purpose.

YOUNG AMERICA'S PATRIOTISM.

Fifth or Sixth Grade.

A short sketch for four or more boys. Let this be given with
ease and boyish spirit.

CHARACTERS.

JAMES. FRANK. JOE. ALBERT.

James. Say Frank, do you know that Washington's birthday is almost here and the teachers all want us to sing a song or tell a story or something, and I just *hate* to speak.

Frank. Well, I don't like it very well myself, but I tell you what it is, James, a fellow has just *got* to show some respect for the Father of His Country, and I think Washington was a regular *brick.* Here comes Joe. (Enter Joe.) Say Joe, what are you going to do for the fellow who was "first in war, first in peace, and first in the hearts of his countrymen."

Joe. Well, I'd like to have a lot of fellows fixed up like soldiers of the Continental army, and make a big show of going to lick the British, as the old colonists did when Washington showed the red coats what Yankee grit was.

James. Well, it did take a lot of grit to go through the hardships the soldiers endured at Valley Forge, and to cross the Delaware that time when the ice was likely to smash their boats and—

Frank. (Clapping him on the shoulder.) Yes! And *you* haven't grit enough to speak a piece for your country. Guess we might do that much, if those grand old heroes could fight and suffer and die for our freedom; I never thought of it in just this way before, but when we consider what those noble patriots did for us, we ought to be proud and happy and willing to show our respect and love for them, by doing the best we can in our line of duty, if it isn't carrying a gun.

Joe. Good! Frank, you are quite right. Here comes Albert with those flags he was to get for our new song. (Albert enter.)

Albert. Here you are, fellows. Hurrah for the stars and stripes! Hurrah for the flag that floats around the world! Come on, here are the rest of the boys. (Enter six or ten boys.) Before we take in the flags let's practice the song. (Boys fall into line.) Already now, one! two! three! (All sing. Air, Marching through Georgia.)

> George Washington, the leader grand
>   Of the army brave and true,
> Fighting for their liberty, they won it grandly, **too.**
>   Now the patroit army cheered
> When all the strife was through,
>   Washington led them on to victory.

Hurrah! Hurrah! for General Washington,
Hurrah! Hurrah! for the glorious cause they
won,
Their fame shall ne'er diminish while the
Union stands as one—
America so free and so noble.

Though few and weak in numbers,
But with spirit staunch and strong,
Struggling bravely for the right,
They pushed their cause along.
Now their fame and glory
We all tell with praise and song,
For Washington led them on to victory.

Boys form military march, if desired, at close of song.

FOR DEWEY DAY, OR ANY PATRIOTIC PROGRAM.

Exercises for Sixth, Seventh or Eighth Grades.

These exercises have been successfully developed for "Dewey Day" in several of the largest grammar schools in Chicago. The marching spirit is developed in " Tramp, Tramp, Tramp," and the modern Dixie introduces the easy swing of the darkey melodies.

A SUCCESSFUL MARCHING EXERCISE WITH SONG.

Boys' Suits to be of the Blue " Dewey " Style—Blue Caps.

AIR—" Tramp, Tramp, Tramp."

When they sunk our gallant Maine,
In the darkness of the night,
And our noble boys were hastened to their graves,
Then the cry came loud and clear,
" We will for their memory fight,
And the starving, struggling people we will save."

> Tramp! Tramp! Tramp! the boys are marching,
> Tho' our hearts were filled with pain,
> And the cry went full and strong over hill and
> over plain,
> We " remember, yes remember, boys, the
> Maine!"

Bravely onward then they marched
'Mid the deadly summer heat,
And they sounded loud the haughty tyrant's knell;
And we shouted loud with joy
When the news of Dewey came,
(Wave caps, shout, hurrah!)
And the day that Santiago lowly fell.

On, on, on the fleet went sailing,
　Caught the Spaniards on the sea,
Sunk their fleet beneath the wave,
Tried their drowning crew to save,
　While they floated high the banner of the free.

And when all the strife was done,
Then our boys came marching home;
From the bitter war and bloodshed now they rest.
They have freed their neighbor weak,
They have cast aside his chain,
And the Stars and Stripes float free from east to west.

　　Tramp! Tramp! Tramp! Our glorious army,
　　　With this banner bright unfurled,
　　We have crossed the wide, wide sea,
　　We have made a people free,
　　　And our banner proudly floats around the world.

SONG FOR "DEWEY DAY," MODERN DIXIE.

AIR—"DIXIE."

Given with great success at Richard Yates and Chase Schools.

(Boys march with high forward step.)

Hi!　Dis am truly a great nation,
Tell you what, beats all creation,
　Look away, look away, at dis united land.
Now norf or souf don't cut no figgah,
Tell you what I'se a happy niggah,
　Look away, look away at dis united land.

Cho.—De norf and souf together, Hooray! Hooray!
 Dey join de forces blue and grey
 And dey lick de Spainyard ebbry day,
  Look away! Look away, look away at our
   great nation!
  Look away! Look away, look away!
  She beats creation.

Ole Spain came in for to lick Uncle Sammy
Found his guns too mighty handy,
 Look away! Look away! At dis united land.
For when his cannons start to tunder
Foreign foes must stand from under,
 Look away! Look away! At dis united land.

Cho.—

Oh! Dixie land she love de banner,
Shows it now in ebbery manner,
 Look away! Look away! At dis united land.
On land and sea around de world, sir,
See Old Glory bright unfurled, sir,
 Look away! Look away! At dis united land.

Cho.—

Ole Glory floats above us, Hooray! Hooray!
 Ole Spain she does not love us,
 Udder nations dare not shove us,
Look away! Look away! Look away at our
 Old Glory!
Look away! Look away! Our banner tells
 de story.

JUBILEE OF PEACE.

The victory's won.   The foe cries; Peace!
And kneeling, conquered, sheaths the sword.
The booming guns on land or sea,
That ceaseless in the conflict roared,
Are silent now, and homeward bound
Come gallant lads with laurels crowned.

A victory blest!   A blessed peace.   The cruel wrongs
        of heavy years,
The grinding chains of slavery are vanquished,
Liberty appears.   Fair Liberty, whose beauteous form
No stain of cruel tyrant mars,
Spreads o'er the struggling people now
Her sheltering wings, 'neath stripes and stars!

Hail, gallant lads on land or sea
Who bared the sword in pity's name,
And for thy suffering brother weak,
With conquering force and courage came.
All honor, to your noble hearts,
All honor, to your wounds and scars,
All honor, to each brave who fought
And rallied to the stripes and stars.

To each dear son who leaped in haste,
In answer to the call "To arms!"
Who gave their lives in breathless heat,
And 'mid the dreadful war's alarms,
Who sank beneath the leaden fire,
In dreary camp and open plain,
We give our tender heart felt prayers,
With saddened memories of the Maine.

KITE DRILL.

Third and Fourth Grade.

A new and pretty exercise for program work. A Drill for twelve boys; wide straw hats, white waists; six kites made of tissue paper—two white, two red, two blue. One line of boys carry kites and string ; march time is used. More boys may be used, so the number is even.

Six boys enter, on the run, carrying kites high in right hand, string in left; march to front of stage; sit on floor; take out "tail" for kite and fasten it on in sixteen beats; rise. Enter other six boys. First boys lift kites above heads; join in line across stage front, kites on one side; march in two circles, meet at back. Forward by twos, face front, halt. Lines face each other. Boys with kites hand them to opposite boys; hold string in right hand; lines separate with backward step, march to stage sides; boys hold kites high in right hand; hold eight counts.

Lines advance, boy winding in string; meet in center. Boys with kites march backward to side; boys with string follow, facing, until both lines are at left stage side.

Boys with kites raise them high in right hand; boys with string face right, run to right side of stage; sixteen counts.

Turn, wind in string; boys meet in line at stage center; boys without kites march off stage; boys with kites march to right side, take off string, put it in pocket. Re-enter boys with kites, like first six; all march to line in front, backward step march, holding kites high, in right hand; form in ranks of three—red, white, blue. Divide into four lines, facing front—three in each line. Use eight counts on all movements. Carry kite by the joining of sticks at back.

Forward lunge with right foot, right hand raised to right, over head, with kite.

Forward lunge with left foot, left hand up, swing from right to left, slowly.

Kneel; face partner; hold kite over face.

Kneel; face partner, hold kite over head.

Rise; groups of three join points of kites in colors—red, white, blue. Pose.

Hold kite on breast; march to single file; exit.

Kites should be about one and a half feet in length. This drill is effective for summer exercise.

THE BUSY BOYS OF UNCLE SAM.

Second or Third Grade.

Exercise for sixteen boys. Costumes, Brownie overalls and close caps. Four boys carry shovels; four, trowels; two with hammers; two with saws; four with paint pails and brushes. March on stage by twos—Divide by twos at stage center front—March to rear. Join ranks of four—shovels in front—trowels next—Carpenters next—painters last.

SING—Air, "Yankee Doodle."

Oh! We're the boys of Uncle Sam, we help to make
　　the nation.
We always like our part to take in every celebration.

CHO.—With the shovel, trowel and saw,
　　　　With hammer and with nails, sir,
　　　　We built our houses good and strong,
　　　　Not one of us e'er fails, sir.

First four make motion of shoveling in time to their singing—four singing.

First we come with shovels, sir,
　　And dig our cellar deep, sir,
To make the building firm and strong.
　　We help along a heap, sir.

Shoulder shovels, march to line in back. This brings masons in front. Four masons sing and act.

The masons now with trowel and stone,
　　Are building up the wall, sir.
We make the house so tall and true,
　　And it will never fall, sir.
　　　　March to line in back.

Four carpenters.

> The carpenters with saws so sharp,
> With hammer and with nails, sir,
> We fix the inside nice and trim,
> From floor to topmost rail, sir.
> March to line in back.

Four painters.

> The painters come with brush and pail,
> To fix the outside bright, sir.
> When we are through we'd have you know
> Our house is all just right, sir.

All together.

> We're building houses every day,
> But not with saw and hammer.
> We build a house of knowledge true,
> And try to like our grammar.

Concert drill.—March time. Each movement eight counts.

Salute.—Carry tool in left hand, raise right hand to forehead with four counts. Lower with four counts.

Present.—Hold tool vertically in front, right hand grasp tool below left. Painters carry pail in left, brush in right. Return to right shoulder, left hand at side.

Lunge right.—Step right, bend knee. Raise right hand, hold eight counts.

Lunge left. Same movement as right.

12 o'clock—Dinner.—Boys march out—get tin pails—march in—seat on stage groups of fours. Sixteen counts—rise—shoulder tools—carry pails—exit.

MOTHER GOOSE'S BOYS.

An exercise for ten small boys dressed in appropriate costumes.
Characters—One little host, Jack Be Nimble, Tommy Tucker,
Boy Blue, Simple Simon, Jack Horner, King Cole and three at-
tendants.

Stage clear. Enter host.

> I am going to have a visit
>   From some charming little men.
> I think you all will know them
>   When you see them coming in.

Enter Jack Be Nimble jumping over candle stick—Shake hands
with host.

Jack Be Nimble.

> Now I am Jack the Nimble,
>   And I am Jack the Quick.
> Just watch me for a minute,
>   While I jump this candle stick.

Enter Tommy Tucker with large slice of bread—Shake hands
etc.

> And I am Tommy Tucker,
>   With a piece of bread and butter,
> And this is how I dance about
>   While waiting for my supper.

Hops about in lively manner.

42

Horn blows outside. Enter Boy Blue, blowing.

Now hear my horn!
Don't you know me,
I am little brave Boy Blue,
And slept like this beside the stack,
While the sheep and cows went through.

Lies down and goes to sleep.

All boys laugh and point to Simple Simon as he enters.

And I am Simple Simon,
Who met the funny pie man,
And fished this way in mother's pail
On that fine day to catch a whale.

Sits down and uses hook and line to fish in a serious way from large pail.

Enter Jack Horner and all except sleeping Boy Blue clap hands.

My name I needn't tell you
When you see this great big pie.
Aint I a smart Jack Horner?
What a great, great boy am I!

Holds up plum.

Music outside. Enter King Cole with crown—Red robe of cheap material—Walks in a stately manner to front—Boy Blue wakes.

Host. Now here's King Cole. (All bow low).

King Cole.

Upon my soul—
Don't I look well and hearty.
Just listen while I call my men
To come here to this party.

Host places chair for King Cole who sits and calls—

Bring in my pipe.

Enter boy and hand pipe.

Bring in my bowl.

Same boy goes to fetch bowl.

Bring in my fiddlers three.

Boy ushers in three fiddlers who enter playing.   Any imitation of fiddles can be used.

All sing to the air, "Merrily We Roll Along."

We're the boys of Mother Goose, Mother Goose,
    Mother Goose,
We're the boys of Mother Goose,
    And nothing e'er shall fret us.
And well we know the children dear, children dear,
    children dear,
Well we know the children dear
    Will never more forget us.

All circle the stage.   Jack Be Nimble leading, jumping over the candle stick as he goes—All act parts as they follow—Exit.

ROLLING PIN DRILL.

Little Bakers.

Movement song and drill for twelve or more small girls—White caps, red dresses, white aprons with long pocket on left side to hold pin when not in use.

Air—"Thumbkin says I'll Dance."
March directly into line for song.

We are baker girls, with our caps and curls,
   With our pins and aprons clean.
Nicest bakers ever seen.
   Place pins in pocket.

Action of kneading.
First we mix our dough,
Kneading it just so,
Work it hard and work it long
Singing sweet our little song.

Rise slowly to tip toes with out spread hands.
Let it rise up light,
Soft and smooth and white.
Puffy, sweet and tender too
Is this bread we bake for you.

Take pins, action of rolling slowly.
Next we'll roll it so,
Straight and hard and slow.
Make it thin and smooth and good
As each little baker should.

Pins back in pocket—Cut with right hand on left.
Biscuits cut out thus,
Do not make a muss.
Put them in the pans just *so*,
Now into the oven go.

(Any good march.)

Drill.—Carry pins in two hands down front—Eight counts to
present pins—Extend pins vertically, right hand lowest—Carry
pins—Return pin to shoulder—Drop left hand, swing pins. Hold
up in right hand, swing right—left, eight counts. Raise over
head, eight counts. Pins raised right, eight counts. Pins raised
left, eight counts. Pose right, hold eight counts. Pose left, hold
eight counts. Kneel, hold pins over head, eight counts. Rest,
place pin on knee, both hands on top, rest chin on hand, rise.
Pins over head, salute—hold pins over head—exit.

LITTLE SWEEPERS.

A Pretty Drill for Sixteen (or less) Little Girls.

Costumes—Pink dresses, white aprons, pink sweeping caps, small broom and dusting cloth tucked in belt.

March on to stage in straight line at back, face front—sweep front in line marching slowly. (Let each child put earnest action in lines).

Concert.

We are busy little sweepers with our brooms and
dusters clean,
We keep the house as fresh and bright as any
you have seen.
We use our brooms so gently, shake our duster
out with care,
And open wide the windows to let in the pure
fresh air.

First girl. I tell you its a burden
To keep house and do it well.

Second. *I* really am *so* busy
I can't get a breathing spell.

Third. And the mud, and dust, and ashes
That are scattered on the floor,

Fourth. Do really quite exhaust me!
My arms and back are sore.

Fifth. To go over walls and ceilings
Makes your back ache worst of all.

Sixth. And to climb up shaky ladders,
Any moment you may fall.

Seventh.   But there's really no use fretting,
                 For it all has to be done,

Eighth.   Even if it keeps us busy
                 From the morn till set of sun.

Ninth.   Now, my dears, you all are wailing,
                 With the burden of your work,

Tenth.   But you'd feel lots worse about it
                 If you tried your work to shirk.

Eleventh.   From the garret to the cellar
                 We must brush, and scrub, and scour,

Twelfth.   Whether bright the sun is shining,
                 Or the rain clouds o'er us lower.

Thirteenth.   But when all the toil is over,
                 All the bustling and the fuss

Fourteenth.   Then we look with pride about us,
                 When we're through with all the muss.

Fifteenth.   Yes, we're busy little sweepers,
                 But we try with all our might,

Sixteenth.   To sweep before our doorways
                 And fix the world up bright.

Sing together—Air, "See Saw."
Sweeping, sweeping, sweeping up and down,
Sweeping, sweeping, now we will clear off every frown.
Working, working, dusting and toiling so gay,
Happy, happy, we try to be every day.

March.—Line divide in center, eight face left, eight face right—march in two circles, brooms over head, held in both hands horizontally. Join in couples at the back, touching raised brooms forming arch—Rear couple shoulder brooms and march under arch to front, each couple following in turn—Divide into single lines—March to side of stage—Lines face—Kneel—Raise broom over head, pose eight counts—Face front, repeat. March in two circles—Join at back. Cross brush end of broom—Forward by twos. Divide front—Join fours in back—Forward fours. Divide front—Join eight in back—Forward eight. Divide front—Join sixteen in back—Forward sixteen. Remain in line in front, with brooms crossed—Shoulder brooms. Courtesy—Single file—Exit.

OUR NATION'S PRIDE.

Patriotic Reading with Accompaniment of Songs.

Can be given as a solo, or the reader may be assisted by chorus. Girl carry fine large flag, suitable for Decoration Day.

As the glowing summer sun,
Is sinking to the west,
We meet to greet these colors,
Emblem of the truest, best,
Noblest nation that he shines on,
Home of all that's grand and free,
Where'er floats these stars resplendent
Gleam they forth for liberty,
And when'er the nation's children
View "Old Glory" floating fair,
To their hearts and lips this music comes
And breathes forth on the air—

"Oh! say can you see, by the dawn's early light
What so proudly we hailed in the twilight's last
      gleaming—
Whose broad stripes and bright stars, through the
      perilous fight,
O'er the ramparts we watched, where so gallantly
      streaming."

Yes; the dear star spangled banner!
How the sight does thrill and cheer,
As under its great strength we rest

And never doubt or fear,
For its grandeur held the nation,
Her sons would not let it fall,
They fought and bled and died for it,
And raised the glorious call—

"The Union forever, hurrah, boys, hurrah,
Down with the traitor, and up with the stars,
For we'll rally round the flag, boys, we'll rally once
    again,
Shouting the battle cry of freedom."

Come we now too late for glory?
No! With us the great charge lies,
To glorify this noble flag,
And hold it near the skies,
Revere and love and cherish it,
And the freedom that it signs
And flourish its bright colors,
Where'er oppression grinds.

"Her mandates make heroes assemble,
When liberty's form stands in view,
Her banners make tyranny tremble,
When borne by the red, white and blue."

The brave youth of America
Must keep the standard high.
Our sons for it may never more
Be forced to fight and die;
But should its stars be menaced,
Or its clear hues bear a stain
Again we'll find they'll rally
From the hill side and the plain—

For the children will be loyal
They will love and guard its might
They will cherish all its stories,
They will keep its colors bright,
And its fame will ne'er diminish,
Its prestige ne'er grow old,
And forever we will chant its praise
With voices free and bold—

"Then conquer we must
For our cause it is just,
And this be our motto, 'In God is our trust.'
And the Star Spangled Banner
Forever shall wave,
O'er the land of the free
And the home of the brave.

—Maude M. Jackson.

MEMORIAL DAY.

Exercise for Eleven Boys, Age 8 to 10 Years.

Letters may be used if desired, placed on top of flag staff.

Air—"Rally Round the Flag."

Come boys, today we'll tell the tale
  Of heroes brave and true,
Who gave this happy land its glorious freedom,
  For we love to tell the story and give honor to
    the brave,
Who shouted the "Battle cry of Freedom!"

M

Recite.

Many were the sons and fathers
  Who marched bravely off to war,
Many fell on field of battle,
  Some returned with many a scar.

E

Everyone of these brave heroes,
  We give love and homage due,
Praise and honor to the dear sons,
  Who saved our grand union true.

M

May the children always love them,
  And remember on this day,
How they marched to drum and bugle,
  To the fight so far away.

O

On the battle field we see them,
  Striving for the banner bright,
Equal rights, true justice ever,
  Fought they grandly for the right.

R

Round this glorious flag they rallied
  Forward with their battle cry,
"Union for ever—ever!"
  Never can their glory die.

I

In the wildest, strongest struggle
  Ever made in freedom's name,
These dear soldiers whom we honor,
  Saved our union! Great their fame!

A

As today the boys remember,
  How these patriots firm and strong,
Stood for all that's free and noble,
  We will praise them loud and long.

L

Lincoln, grand and loving hearted
  We fore'er his name shall chant,
Honor Sheridan! Honor Sherman!
  Honor give to General Grant!

D

Do you think the nation's children
  Will forget their noble dead?
Nay! We'll ever cherish fondly,
  Those whose precious blood was shed.

A

And around this starry banner
　We will rally with fond hearts,
Loyal ever to its standard,
　And the truth its strength imparts.

Y

Yes! we'll hold it firm and steady,
　Proudly 'neath its folds we stand,
May it float in deathless glory,
　O'er the schools in all our land.

Cho.—And we'll march beneath the banner,
　　And we'll love its colors bright,
　Over our schools 'twill float forever.
　　We'll remember all the heroes,
　Who fought nobly for the right,
　　Praising their honored names forever!
　The Union forever, hurrah boys, hurrah!
　　Here is our banner, and bright with many
　　　a star,
　And we'll rally round the flag boys,
　　And ever love the right,
　Over our schools 'twill float forever!

DECORATION DAY.

Exercise for Twelve Girls 8 to 10 Years.

Letters may be used if desired, but flowers are sufficient.

Air—"Hurrah for the Brave Old Flag."

Today we bring the flowers
    In freshest garlands here,
In memory of our noble dead,
    Who saved our country dear,
And all the dainty blossoms,
    A meaning sweet doth tell,
To show our love and honor,
    For the brave who fought so well.

D

Recite.

I bring the pretty daisy,
    And with the token bright,
I honor give to the dear sons,
    Who struggled for the right.

E

The Evergreen shows constancy,
    And we will ever bring
Our tender tribute to our dead,
    And earnest praises sing.

C

The Cedar shows "Allegience"
A worthy thought and true,
For by this spirit these brave men,
Saved our "Red, White and Blue."

O

The Oak leaves green and glossy,
Will make a garland fair,
To rest upon the soldier's grave,
For love and reverence there.

R

White Roses sweet and fragrant,
Mean freedom glad and grand,
And these dead heroes nobly gave
Their lives for our dear land.

A

This spray of Arbor Vitæ,
Shows friendship firm and pure,
And may it reach from north to south,
And thus for aye endure.

T

This Tuberose is a lovely thought,
Appreciation true,
And well becomes this honored day,
When we brave deeds review.

I

Blue Iris means "A Messenger,"
Ah! Let us hope 'twill be,
A messenger of love and peace,
And symbol of the free.

O

Oleander cries "Beware!"
  A warning may we heed,
Let love and justice ever rule,
  Let warriors no more bleed.

N

Nasturtium, rich in many a hue,
  We bring in love and pride,
To deck the grave of noble sons,
  Who for their country died.

D

Here is the humble Dandelion,
  Whose brilliant yellow crest,
Creeps here and there in living gold,
  To crown the soldier's rest.

A

"Honor in age" the Almond means,
  How beautiful the way
To bring this thought home to our hearts,
  On our "Memorial Day."

Y

Yellow roses sweet I bring,
  Bright and fresh and fair to see,
For the stalwart sturdy sons,
  Who died for equal liberty.

Come one, come all, and leave your garlands here,
  In honor of our noble sons,
Sing praises loud and clear.
  Hurrah, hurrah, for equal rights hurrah,
Hurrah for the brave old flag,
  That bears the stars and stripes.

Each girl carry flag in left hand, letter fastened on the breast.

PATRIOTIC PANORAMA.

Seventh and Eight Grades.

A sketch of historic events. Introducing early American history and events to the present day. Supported by songs, flag-drill, readings and living pictures. Principal speaker introduces various numbers. Time, thirty minutes.

First Speaker. My country, "The gem of the ocean, the home of the brave and the free." On this day, set apart as the soldiers' Sabbath, well may our hearts be filled with praise and reverence for thy honored dead.

Come, with swelling voices and loyal hearts, to do homage to these noble souls who gave their lives that we might enjoy the blessings of a land of liberty.

(Enter 16 or 24 girls in white costumes, with small flag on shoulder, or sash of red and blue. Sing, Columbia the Gem of the Ocean. Columbia behind draped curtain made of two large flags. Let curtain be drawn aside revealing Columbia in pose as girls sing. Speaker pass to side and sit during song).

(Speaker resume). Four centuries ago the gallant Genoese sailor, seeking the far East, first gave to civilization the wonderful news of a

new world.   Little did the incredulous old world
dream, that within five hundred years, this almost mythical portion of the great unknown
would dominate the Eastern hemisphere with a
masterful influence.

(Columbus taking position back of curtain.
Pose as if looking far ahead).

Looking backward we see, on that spring
morning, Columbus landing upon the shores of
San Salvador, looking with amazement and reverent awe at this wonderful fertile land.   Columbia, thy name may well honor the noble adventurer whose faith and energy disclosed this
country to the ignorant world.   (Curtain fall).
With tender reverent hearts do we turn to those
intrepid souls, whose strong natures revolted
against the old world tyranny, and, venturing all
their hopes to the unknown West, landed at
Plymouth Rock.   (Curtain drawn.   Four Puritans in costumes—two boys, two girls.   Pose in
attitude of devotion while poem is recited).   The
well known words of our poet aptly describes
this dreary scene of the gloomy landing of the
Pilgrim Fathers.   (Enter girl and recite poem of
Mrs. Hemans, "The breaking waves etc").

Speaker.   The same spirit of sturdy independ-
ence which prompted the Pilgrims to flee from
the despotic East, incited the Colonists to throw

off the galling yoke of tyrannical taxation. Braving the danger of trial for treason, the gallant band in Boston enacted the determined scene of the Boston Tea Party.

(Curtain drawn. Four boys in Indian suits. Two boxes of tea, hatchets, etc. Pose while one girl sings three verses of song to tune of Yankee Doodle Dandy.

> "I'll drink no tea, dear sir," said he
> Yankee Doodle Dandy.

Columbia on this day gives honored tribute to the stalwart soldiers who starved and suffered in the dreary camp át Valley Forge and, with deep prayers of thankfulness, breathes the sacred name of Washington. (Curtain reveals Washington in Continental uniform, yellow and blue). We see him at the close of one of the grandest struggles ever made in Freedom's name, receiving the surrender of Cornwallis. (Cornwallis extends sword to Washington. British suit of scarlet and white. Two pose, while chorus of boys enter and sing, "Hail Columbia," "Sound, sound the tramp of," etc.) How the memory of that important event rings in the stirring words of (enter boys) ("Sound," etc.)

America sadly, yet proudly on this 30th of May, bows in heartfelt sorrow and gratitude over the graves of the boys in blue who thirty-eight years ago, marched boldly forth under the rippling folds of Old Glory.

The fields of Gettysburg, Shiloh, Chattanooga and Look Out Mountain bear witness on this sacred day of the nation's remembrance.

(Introduce here any appropriate recitation; "Bay Billy," "Home Sweet Home," or any preferred selection).

Speaker.   To-day Columbia bends in homage as we "Cover them over with beautiful flowers." (Enter twelve girls with flowers and sing, "Cover them over with beautiful flowers," etc.)   (Columbia, with soldiers at "Parade Rest." Columbia kneel during song).

But one brief year ago, the battle cry of "Rally Round the Flag Boys" again echoed from shore to shore of our vast empire, and this time North and South united under the starry banner, went forth to aid humanity's cause and strike again the glorious blow for the freedom of a struggling people.

Columbia's sons sprang ready to defend her honor and her flag and gave their lives to crush another tyrant's cruel cause.   On the hills of El Caney, at Santiago, at Manila in the far Orient, the boys in blue thundered the proclamation of Freedom and to-day our mingled pride and grief places loving garlands o'er the sleeping heroes, as we sadly

"Remember the Maine."

(Tableau—soldier, sailor with anchor—Columbia kneel).

Over the warriors of a century ago, up to the present day, our fragrant tributes will be laid as the lesson of their noble sacrifice for Country is borne upon our minds. (Columbia and new countries pose until close of piece).

Columbia's flag now floats around the world, and in her sheltering arms she holds the feeble, oppressed and ignorant. (Enter flag-drill of 16 to 24 girls). She will raise them to the full appreciation of what this glorious Star Spangled Banner means to mankind, and our heroes will not have died in vain. (Sing Star Spangled Banner).

Final Group.—Flag-drill march to back. Columbia march to stage center. Sailor and soldier on right. Columbus, Puritans on left. Washington and Cornwallis on right. Boston Tea Party, left. Chorus at back, sing "America."

CARNIVAL OF THE MUSES.

Suitable for Commencement Work. Eighth Grade.

SYNOPSIS.

Euterpe, goddess of Music, and Thespia, goddess of Drama, summon Flora, goddess of Flowers, Ceres, goddess of Harvest, Persephone, daughter of Ceres, and Diana, goddess of the Chase, to a Carnival of Song and Story; Helen of Troy and Cleopatra are also invited. The goddess of Fate appears. These two mortals implore Fate to tell for them the distant future. Fate complies and brings before them the events and great characters of the coming centuries even to the present day. Time one hour.

CAST OF CHARACTERS:

Music, EUTERPE. Two attendants in Greek gowns.

Drama, THESPIA.

FLORA. Six attendants with flowers, etc.

CERES. Wreath of poppies and wheat.

PERSEPHONE.

DIANA. Carry silver bow and arrow.

FATE. Pale grey suit in Greek design.

CLEOPATRA,

HELEN OF TROY,

ISABELLA, Queen of Spain,

PATRICK HENRY,

GODDESS OF LIBERTY,

WASHINGTON,

LAFAYETTE,

JOAN OF ARC,

NAPOLEON,

WELLINGTON,

QUEEN TITANIA,

KING OBERON,

SOLDIER,

SAILOR,

Greek goddesses to wear the Greek gowns. Other characters, the costumes suitable to characters.

Stage arranged with seats at back, covered with drapery of dark color. Arrange for fourteen seats. Let good music accompany exits and entrances. As characters finish posing, group at the back near the music.

(Music. Euterpe enter, accompanied by two attendants.)

Euterpe. A fair and tender evening. My whole soul is filled with the ecstacy of music. (Enter Thespia.) A royal greeting to you. I have been thinking of you and pondering upon the mystery of Fate. Although immortal, I look forward into the distant ages for some sign of the future, but all is blank.

Thespia. Let us summon our dear associates and have a carnival of song and story, and maybe we can tempt Fate to reveal to us the future.

Euterpe. Your thought is mine. (To attendants:) Go you to Flora, Ceres and Diana, say to them we would greet them here. (Exit attendants.)

Thespia. Shall we summons any mortals?

Euterpe. I fancy it would be fitting to bring among us the two most beautiful women the world has known—Helen of Troy and Cleopatra.

Thespia. Distinct in type of loveliness, their impress upon history is imperishable. (Music. Enter Flora with attendants, Diana, Ceres, Persephone. All bow low three times as group advances.)

Euterpe. Dear and gentle sisters, a cordial welcome to you. On this fair eve it is fitting that the beloved members of our ancient and powerful circle should meet for a joyful carnival. Think you not, future times and future thought will bear an indelible impress of our mighty power? Thespia, bid our sisters welcome.

Thespia (bowing low). Twice and thrice welcome! We of immortal fame are not of the present, but of the past and future. I feel, nay know, that these beautiful stories of our beloved Greeks and Romans will be a never-failing source of interest and instruction to the future youth. To-day I, as goddess of the drama, foretell, that through its influence the education, the elevation of the mass of the people will be developed. From the beginning of the history of mankind have the people sought rest and instruction, and expansion tnrough the medium of action, song and story. In no more forcible manner can truth be presented. To me mankind owes a deep debt of gratitude.

Flora. Nobly said! You give to the mind what I bring to the sight and nostrils of men. In my train is brightness, lightness, perfume and beauty. I can foresee how all nature throughout the ages rejoice in my beauty and power. I can, indeed, hear the songs and see the devotion given my lovely flowers. Even as I speak the words of a dainty mortal singing in sweetest tones do I hear. I will repeat it for you. (Sings, "Come Buy My Flowers," by C. A. White). Does she not pay earnest tribute to my power? "Emblems of faith, friendship and love so true." Ah! that covers the whole range of human and immortal affection.

Ceres. How glad am I to be with you! How happy when I spread my arms over the earth and its fruitfulness feeds the children of men. Goddess of Harvest am I, and blessed, indeed. And Persephone, dear Persephone, whom the dark God of Hades had stolen from me, is returned to me this day. (Persephone kneels at Ceres' side.)

Diana. I am also happy; although I love the chase and care little for companionship, I am truly glad to be of your number. Are mortals to be among us? (Music outside.)

Euterpe. The two most beautiful women of the time are here. (Enter Cleopatra and Helen of Troy. All bow low except Cleo.)

Thespia. To such famous mortals we bow in glad welcome.

Cleo. Most gracious muses! You are alone! Where are the gods? Where is Marc Antony?

Helen. We passed a company of youth and men upon the road. They were singing, evidently going or returning from the Olympian games.

Euterpe. They *have* been to the games. We shall not be behind them in exercise and physical culture. Will the future women and girls follow the steps of our Spartan or Roman womenkind? Ah! The future! Come, join in one of our harmonies.

Thespia. Gladly. You will all assent?

Cleo. I will but watch you. That will be the greater pleasure. (Cleo. and Helen pass to back and sit.)

(Thespia, Euterpe, Diana, Ceres, Flora, Persephone join in line at back for Delsarte exercise.)

Thespia. We are ready. (Music for exercise.)

Ceres. Now, while we rest, Euterpe, thou dear friend of humanity, let us listen. (Leads music to front. Introduce any pretty classical solo here.)

Euterpe. With pleasure. (Sings.)

Diana (listening). (All lean forward in attitude of expectation and half fear). I hear a soft, but resolute foot-step. My ears, trained for the chase, are keen to catch the faintest sound. Listen, hear the slow and solemn music. (Group together—Cleo. advances to front of group—Fate enters to left.)

Persephone. I am filled with a vague fear! Whom can it be thus approaching? What dreadful presence is near us? (Leans on Ceres).

Euterpe. Whom can this be? (Fate advances to front).

Cleopatra. The Goddess of Fate! (All bow very low.)

Thespia. We welcome you, most reverenced and awful of our circle. Unto you we turn for the future.

Cleo. (Advancing). Ah! Read for us the future! With your mystic spell withdraw the veil of destiny. Who in future years shall equal Marc Antony, this beautiful Helen or myself?

Helen. As mortals we cannot see the future as can these beauteous Muses. On this fair night, we implore thee, mighty mistress of the destinies of men, show to us the future of mankind. My eager soul tries in vain to pierce the heavy darkness of advancing years. The future, ah! read for us the mighty future.

Fate. Ah! Rash impatient souls, your fate is written upon your fair faces! Alas! That I should see the dark destiny to which your beauty hastens you!

Cleo. Tell us not of that! Into the distant centuries cast your dreadful soul, and reveal to us the nature of future civilization.

Fate. Be it so! So mighty, so potent is this mysterious power, that I will bring before your eyes the scenes of future progress. (All sit at rear of stage).

From century to century do I see men struggling, fighting, nations rising and falling, empires created and destroyed. Through all the conflict and bloodshed I see the soul of liberty growing stronger and stronger. Wonderful to reveal, I see an ambitious soul proclaiming a new and startling theory of the earth's shape. All the world is incredulous. A gracious, generous woman aids the courageous adventurer, a queen of a newer civilization, her name Isabella. Behold she is revealed to you. (Enter Isabella—speaks). To womankind must the nations of the earth give deepest homage, for through the nobleness of woman has civilization advanced. (Euterpe leads Isabella to rear).

Fate. Into the far, far west does my gaze extend. I see a vast new continent, peopled by a powerful race who form a nation which dominates the world. Among this people has arisen, out of the past, new philosophies, sciences and a new literature. The achievements of our Greeks and Romans are regarded as the curious history of an ancient age. To the uttermost part of the earth does the influence of this mighty nation extend. Intelligent, progressive in mind and body, I see the youth poring over the stories of our noble athletes.

Upon the shores of this continent the fairest goddess of all ages has risen in her majestic beauty. (Enter Liberty). Liberty, in thy grandeur, thou hath found an eternal and congenial home.

Liberty.

> A home at last! Beneath these skies
> Where freedom's flag triumphant flies.
> No stain its glorious beauty mars,
> Resplendent shine its glittering stars.
> Beneath its folds my soul finds rest,
> As, floating free from east to west,
> It bears upon its folds of light
> To all the world its message bright.
> Glad freedom! Home of liberty!
> Columbia, my soul in thee
> Is blended with thy glorious might,
> Where wrong is vanquished by the right.
> Here in thy sheltering arms find rest
> Humanity with wrongs oppressed.
> Almighty nation! On thy shore
> My soul shall rest forevermore!

Euterpe. As an immortal, I welcome you among us. Even if thou art of the future, thy soul has been alive throughout the ages. To

thee, fairest goddess of time and eternity, to thee
we accord the highest place (all bow), the greatest honor.   (Liberty sit on high seat at rear.)

Fate.   Within this land, this home of liberty,
I see the people awakening.   I hear the masterful voice of a great champion ringing clear.   Behold a noble orator, even as those of our time;
the name, Patrick Henry, and his eloquence
startling the people to action.

(Enter Patrick Henry—Repeat part of famous
speech).

Fate.   I see the birth of the young nation.   At
its head is placed a noble general; a follower of
our great god, Mars, only because it is the one
way to deliver his people.   I hear a grateful
nation breathing the name of Washington.   Beloved is he, even as Cæsar.

Across the waste of waters sounds this conflict
and other nations of the world look upon the
struggle with amazement, some with sympathy.
A noble man of a distant empire hears the call
and feels the need of his suffering brother.   Lafayette, of a country called France, speeds to the
aid of the cause of liberty.   Side by side stand
these grand men, Washington and Lafayette,
representing the union in spirit of the love of
liberty.   Washington, the father of a country

where liberty and equal rights bring womankind into high honor.

Even as our Spartan maidens strive for a sound mind in a sound body, equally do the maidens of this distant country develop their physical forces. (Here can be introduced any physical culture drill by 12 or 16 girls.)

Fate. Other empires and nations will be guided and ruled by women through these future centuries. Even this land of the noble Lafayette will be saved through the leadership and divine inspiration of a slender maiden, who has been im. pelled by a mysterious power, greater than any power possessed by our gods. (Enter Joan of Arc.) Joan of Arc leads a vast army in successful battle.) (Pose with uplifted sword.)

Fate. The years pass. Another leader of this same people rises. Even as Alexander does his ambitions lead him o'er broken oaths and through a sea of blood to victory after victory. I see him addressing his army. I hear him called Napoleon, the greatest general of the nineteenth century. He sweeps on and on! But, ah! he reaches the climax. A powerful nation, even as the Persians, oppose him. On a vast battlefield, called Waterloo, Wellington, the great English general, hurls the French back with crushing defeat. This terrible battle decides the destinies of millions.

You are weary of warfare. Ah! "War is a terrible trade, but in the cause of the righteous sweet is the sound of the conflict."

But I will tell you of newer legends. The childish mind in these times is satisfied with the tales of our gods and goddesses. But a daintier, more fanciful people have been created for these future children. They are called wonderful bright fairies and elves. So light, so pretty, so pure! I will bring them to you. Their queen, Titania, their king, Oberon. (Enter fairies, dance together. Titania sings "Home of the Fairies," by C. A. White.)

Fate. You would have a brief glance at this new home of this beauteous goddess. Her honor and her flag are protected by a gallant band who reverence our god of the sea, Neptune. Vast ships of a vast navy float her flag around the world. On land the army guard her shores and the people chant a glad, new anthem, "The Army and Navy Forever, Three Cheers for the Red, White and Blue."

The prophecy endeth here. I hold in my hand all the future of time. My commands are absolute. Muses, pass thee to thy several ways. (Muses pass softly off stage.) Mortals, fulfill thy destinies! (Characters pass. Liberty remains at rear.)

Fate. At thy feet, sweet Liberty, dearest beloved of all (kneels) I bow in adoration, for thy spirit raises humanity to its highest development and civilizes the earth. (Pose sixteen counts. Music, Stars and Stripes Forever. Fate passes left, Liberty advances to front, with raised hand. Exit.)

QUEEN OF THE YEAR.

4th, 5th, 6th, or 7th Grades.

Arranged for closing exercises—Short cantata, introducing thirteen actors—Five male and eight female characters.

Costumes—Father Time, Suit of dark gray made in long loose gown belted in at the waist. Sickle in belt and hour glass on small stand at left. Have small raised throne with room for two seats.

Twelve months in costume.

January—Boy of eight or ten years. Three cornered hat. Knee breeches. Lace ruffles at waist and neck.

February—Older boy, as St. Valentine. Dark suit, wide hat, shoulder cape and sack of pretty valentines.

March—Boy, Dull brown suit, yellow hair flying. One long tin horn at belt and one in hand.

April—Girl dressed in pale green. Wide green hat. Sprinkling can in hand.

May—Girl in apple blossom suit of pink and white with flowers.

June—Older girl. Leading character. Loose hair. White gown. Roses.

July—Boy. Red white and blue suit. Five crackers and torpedoes.

August—Yellow suit. Girl with grains.

September—Girl in dark green with fruits.

October—Autumn suit of red, yellow and brown. Girl with basket of nuts.

November—Tall girl in grey. Basket with small pumpkin, etc.

December—Boy. Suit with furs and Christmas toys.

Lines can be spoken or sung as desired. Each month circle the stage as they address Time. Father Time seated on stage. Sings.

Air—"Grandfather's Clock."

Ah! I'm Father Time, I am hoary and old,
And my age there are none who can know,

And they say that I reck not as onward I sweep,
How the months and the years come and go.
But I have in my heart for each month in the year,
An affection both steadfast and true,
As they come, come, each in proper turn,
Until all of the seasons are thro'.

(Voices outside. Speaks.) What wild commotion is this I hear? Enter, enter, friends, what can Father Time do for you. (Enter twelve months singing.)

Air—"Annie Rooney."

Oh! Father Time, we come to you,
Now tell us Father, tell us true,
Of all the months; which one to you
    Is counted as the fairest;
Every one of us today,
Have each our merits here to say,
When we have finished, tell us, pray,
    Which one to you is fairest.

Father Time (chorus to Annie Rooney.)

Each one of you may tell me,
Why you should the fairest be,
Then I'll answer without fear
Which month is the fairest of all the year.

Each month as they speak step forward.
January (Steps forward toward Father Time, kneels).

Good Father Time, you see in me,
    The first of all this merry crowd,

L. of C.

And with my coming every year
   The New Year's Bells ring clear and loud;
I bring fresh courage to each heart,
   With me the resolution strong
That during all the coming year
   Men promise they will not do wrong.
They will not drink or swear or cheat,
   But ways of virtue seek with care,
And to each fellow man the meet,
   Will be so upright, just and fair.

F. Time.

Alas! The firm resolves they make
   To leave their vices great and small,
Too often they at length forsake,
   And then do not improve at all.

February.   (Bow low.)

I represent the second month
   As good St. Valentine;
In February come I then
   With many a tender line,
Which tells love's tale of joy and hope
   With earnest wish expressed.
In many loving hearts
   I am, of all the months, the best.

March.   (Blows horn. Run swiftly about stage.)

Good Father, they call me so rude and so bluff,
My voice is so loud and my ways are so rough,
My sport makes all shiver as a gale from my lips,
Bends over the branches and tosses the ships—
And yet if I came not with roar and with rush

To frighten Jack Frost and turn him to slush,
No milder or warmer or pleasanter breeze,
Would come on to charm them and rustle green leaves.

Father T. (Shakes hands with March.)
Well said, hearty March! Though you're rough and you're
bold,
Your will is right good and your heart is not cold.

April. (Air "Gentle Annie.")
Oh! I come, Father Time, in my beauty,
Fresh and dainty the green that I wear,
And gentle the showers that attend me,
With my smiles and my tears in the air;
Over hillside and meadow and valley,
I trip with a light, airy tread,
And the flowers that were sleeping so soundly
Lift to heaven each fair dainty head—
And Nature rejoices with me,
Though capricious and fitful my ways,
And the children are glad, glad to greet me
And joyously welcome my days.

May. (Dancing gaily.)
With my coming, Father Time,
Apple blossoms bloom again,
Over hill and vale and plain
Robins chant a glad refrain.
Cherry trees and plum and peach
Gayly deck themselves at night;
And the children fondly reach
For these nodding plumes of white.
Glad and gay the songs they sing,
As they dance along the lane,

Happily their voices ring,
"May, dear May has come again."

June.   (Bending low.   Raising roses over head.)

Father Time, I am here in my richness
    Of summer's full beauty and bloom,
Around me the gay roses cluster,
    How sweet is their subtile perfume.
Now all of the hills and the valleys
    Are in their full verdure arrayed,
Earth is fair as the Garden of Eden
    Ere from it our first parents strayed.
The sky is so blue and so tender,
    And love seems abroad in the land;
While beautiful flowers, the roses,
    Rich roses, a flame on each hand.
My name is a dear one to lovers,
    My beauty the poets have sung,
Men's whole hearts are filled with pure rapture,
    When birds in my praises give tongue.

July.   (Air, Marching Through Georgia.
Run about stage.   Throw down torpedoes.)

I come with glad rejoicing and with fervent hope and cheer,
    Celebrated as I am, the best month in the year.
Loudly at my coming does the Nation strongly cheer,
    Though I am hot, dry and dusty,
Hurrah, Hurrah, I bring the glorious Fourth!
    Hurrah, Hurrah, from East and West and North!
Gladly do they celebrate the Independent fourth,
    Though I am hot, dry and dusty.

August. (Air. Bring in the Sheaves.)

Now the harvest coming, Royal August brings it,
  Ripening fields of beauty, rich with yellow grain,
Stories of winter comfort, food for all the Nation;
  Underneath the Dog Star, ripens on plains,
Bringing in the sheaves, bringing in the sheaves,
  We shall come rejoicing bringing in the sheaves.

September. (Basket of fruit.)

Now September onward comes,
Ripened apples, peach and plums,
Hazelnuts and blackhaws sweet,
Gentians blossom at my feet.
Children shout aloud their glee,
In these last days they are free.
Soon will ring the bells for school,
To call them back to rote and rule.
Loudly do they chant my praise
In these last vacation days.
So they think with you and I,
Blessings brighten as they fly.

October. (Basket of nuts—Let them fall from hand to patter).

Rich October's beauty glowing,
All the land seems overflowing
With my stores from wood and field.
In the copse the squirrels chatter
While the nuts fall pit, pit, patter,
As the trees their richness yield.
Gay Jack Frost, the sprightly fellow,
Paints with colors rich and mellow

All the landscape far and wide.
On the oak the crimson's burning,
Brightest yellow beeches turning
By the pleasant river side.

November.

(Air—"When You and I were Young, Maggie.")

Although I am somber and grey, Father,
And leaden my skies overcast,
I have in my brief space of days, Father,
A glad time which ever will last.
It came many long years ago, Father,
And I know it will ne'er pass away,
For the Nation remembers it gladly,
'Tis our good, noble Thanksgiving Day.
For years we've remembered the day, Father,
With turkey and good things galore,
And I know that the old times will last, Father,
Until you and I are no more.

December.

Last of all the year am I,
And I bring much frost and cold,
Grey the year is growing now,
For he's getting very old.
Though the frost nips toes and ears,
Children's voices gaily chime
As they prattle of my joys,
For I bring glad Christmas time.
Loving thoughts to all should come
"Peace on earth, good will toward men."
We have answered each in turn,
Give us your decision then.

Father Time. (Rising).

Now your help I ask together,
Help me judge now, as to whether,
In this contest of bright tune,
We shall not *choose* lovely *June*,
Queen of *all* the year is she
Aud we greet her *royally.*

Father Time advances to meet June, who bows low at the last line. He seats her beside him on throne while the other months sing.

Sing—Air, "Beautiful June." (Bowing low).

Beautiful, beautiful, beautiful June,
Summer has come again, beautiful June.
Beautiful, beautiful, beautiful June,
Summer has come again, beautiful June.

June, rising, sings.

I am here with you once more in my pride,
Sweet are the roses abloom on each side,
Beautiful birds are now singing in tune,
Telling with gladness 'tis beautiful June.

Chorus of all as above.

CHO.

Softly the white clouds float over our heads,
Green is the carpet o'er all the hills spread,
Bright are the meadows with freshest of bloom,
Gay are the roses, and rich with perfume.

So we'll dance gaily this glad holiday,
June is here with us, not long will she stay.
We'll gather the sunshine, it passes so soon,
And still in our hearts, we'll have beautiful June.

Months join right hands—circle singing chorus—join hands in line swinging and swaying as feet are crossed alternately. Make the number light and joyous. Exit.

JUVENILE PANTOMIME.

For Girl and Boy of 10 or 12 years.

By MRS. MAE R. PERKINS.

"COMIN' THRO' THE RYE."

Verse 1.　　　　Gin a body meet a body,
　　　　　　　　Comin' thro' the rye,
　　　　　　　　Gin a body kiss a body,
　　　　　　　　Need a body cry?

Boy. *Lines 1 and 2.* (Walk in, hands at side, meet partner at center of stage. Greet partner and shake hands.)

Lines 3 and 4. (Still holding partner's hand, kneel and kiss it, on line three. Rise on line four, arms extended, face expresses surprise, head shakes as if to say, "don't cry.")

Girl. *Lines 1 and 2.* (Enter with circle step, hands hold skirt and sways in opposition, look at toe, greet partner with pleasant smile and hand shake.)

Lines 3 and 4. (Face expresses surprise at his kissing you, turn to left and cover eyes with hand and begin crying, weight on left foot. Dry your tears and prepare for chorus.)

Chorus.　　　　Ilka lassie has her laddie,
　　　　　　　　Nane, they say, ha'e I;
　　　　　　　　Yet a' the lads they smile at me,
　　　　　　　　When comin' thro' the rye.

Girl. *Lines 1 and 2.* (Lean forward on advanced foot, point several times to self, shake head "Yes." (*2.*) Back on retired foot, holding hand to chest, shake head "No.")

Lines 3 and 4. Hands back of head, head resting on hands and bent to right, look at partner with a rougish smile.)

Boy. *Lines 1 and 2.* (Weight on advanced foot, lean forward, point to self several times, smiles and shakes head "Yes." (*2.*) Weight on retired foot, hand points to partner, face expresses surprise, saying oh! oh!)

Lines 3 and 4. (Take several steps back, at same time pointing to partner, face says "Of course they do.")

Verse 2.   Gin a body meet a body,
                    Comin' frae the town,
                    Gin a body greet a body
                    Need a body frown?

Girl. *Lines 1 and 2.* (Enters or rather crosses further to left of stage with change step, hands on hips. When partner greets you, pass him by with nose up in air.)

Lines 3 and 4. (Stand to right of partner, weight on both feet, hands at side and clenched. Turn head and look at partner several times, face expressing haughtiness.)

Boy. *Lines 1 and 2.* (Walk towards partner, takes hat off and bows.)

Lines 3 and 4. (Looks bewildered, then advances on right foot, both arms extended, oblique front. Face expresses inquiry.)

Chorus.—Repeat.

Verse 3.   Amang the train there is a swain,
                    I dearly lo'e mysel',
                    But what's his name, or where's his hame,
                    I din'na choose to tell.

Girl. *First line.* (Expression of bashfulness, finger to mouth.)
Second line. (Hands on heart, lean forward, express joy.)
Third line. (Use teacher's affirmation of hand and raise eyebrows, a coquettish smile.)
Fourth line. (Arms extended, oblique front, shake head "No.")
Boy. *First line.* (Lean forward, arms extended, face expresses "Is it I?")
Second line. (Emphasize the above.)
Third line. (Advance towards partner in coaxing manner, as much as to say "Oh tell me.")

Chorus.—Repeat first two lines the same as after verses 1 and 2.

Lines 3 and 4. (Girl goes swaying off the stage, passes in front of partner. Just before she reaches exit, she stops and smiles very mischievously at him.

Boy assumes attitude of disappointment.)

TEN DIALOGUES

IN RHYME

FOR PRIMARY SCHOOLS

BY

ALICE TURNER

AND

GERTRUDE SMITH

SUPPLEMENTARY TO

PRACTICAL PROGRAMS.

56555

THE RAILROAD TRAIN.

[FOR SEVEN BOYS.]

———

First Boy [advancing and turning so that he stands with
his face towards the audience]:—

> One is the engine, large and grand,
> That waits for the engineer's command;
> One is the engine, shining and fine,
> That stands at the head of the cars in line.

Second boy [coming forward and standing behind first]:—

> Two is the baggage-car, ready to go,
> Watched by the baggage-men, all in a row;
> Two is the baggage-car, solid and strong,
> That carries the trunks and valises along.

Third boy [ranging himself in line]:

> Three's the express-car, with double locks;
> Send what you please in a parcel or box;
> Three's the express-car, yellow or brown,
> That carries the money from town to town.

Fourth boy [crossing into line]:

> Four is the postal-car.   Letters are here,
> Written by friends to friends who are dear.
> Four is the postal-car, open to all,
> That carries the letters for great and small.

Fifth boy [in line]:

> Five is a passenger-car, just made,
> Upholstered in plush of the latest shade;
> Five is a passenger-car, so gay,
> That carries the people who ride by day.

Sixth boy [in line]:

> Six is a sleeping-car, pleasant sight!
> In comfort and peace you may ride all night.
> Six is a sleeping-car, gorgeous and bright,
> That carries the people who ride by night.

Seventh boy:—

> Seven's a dining-car, charming and cool,
> With tables and chairs and a vestibule.
> Seven's a dining-car, large and neat,
> That carries the people who travel and eat.

All together:—

> This is a train, all ready to go,
> That works for all the world, you know.
> That goes as fast as a bird with wings,
> Clear the track! Clear the track! when the loud
>   bell rings!

MINNA C. SMITH.

WHAT TO DO.

[FOR TWO BOYS.]

———

GEORGE:— A soldier and a sailor,
A merchant and a tailor,
A lawyer and a grocer man,
A doctor. Well, who can
Decide what it is best to be?
Let me see,—
A dry-goods man, base ball,
A tinsmith, a reporter "on call,"
An actor, a salesman, a lumberman,
Well, I must decide if I can.

A sailor has a life that's free;
The world is his to choose;
And though while that a fact may be,
He yet the world may lose.

All men can soldiers be on call,
When needed by their State;
A soldier's life's not mine at all;
I'd rather be a captain tall,
Or else a captain's mate.

I would not be a merchant,
Nor yet a grocer man.
Well, John, what would you be?
Do tell me, if you can.

JOHN:— I think that it would wiser be
Just to wait.
There is much for us to do,
Time is going, that is true;
But each day will surely show
Something needful we should know
For our fate.

Never mind what we may choose,
There'll be much to gain or lose
    Every day.
So you see we can but wait,
Work and study; and our fate—
Be it lawyer or lumberman—
We'll decide it when we can,—
    So I say.

THE ROSEBUD RING.

[FOR SIX GIRLS, EACH ONE WITH A ROSEBUD IN HER HAND.]

KATE [who is a little older and taller than any of the others]:

    Six little girls, and what do you think?
    They live upon nothing but victuals and drink;
    And like the old lady, on this kind of diet
    It's very hard work for them all to be quiet.

The six recite in concert:—

    Six little girls are we, are we,
    All as quiet as can be,
    Except when we laugh, or play, or sing,
    Or dance about in a rosebud ring.

[All join hands and circle round as in the game "Ring around-a-rosy." Then they fall back into line and speak in turn.]

SUSIE:—We have a new game called the Rosebud Ring;
    And when we play it, we laugh and sing;
        We join hands *so,*
        And away we go.

[When Susie says: "We join hands so," she turns to Mamie, who is next to her, and takes Mamie's hand. At the words "Away we go," they go up to Helen.]

MAMIE:— We are rosebuds two;
    And we come to you,
    Just to see
    If it shall be
    Rosebuds three?

[Helen takes Mamie's hand and the three go to Louie.]

HELEN:— Now you see
    We are rosebuds three,
    We want one more.
    Will you be
    Rosebud four?

[All go on to Nellie.]

LOUIE:— Four little rosebuds in a row;
    There ought to be one more, I know.
    Dear little friend, will you come with me,
    That five little rosebuds there may be?

[The five, hand in hand, turn towards Kate.]

NELLIE:— Five little rosebuds waiting here
    For you to come with us, my dear.
    Six is our number, don't you see?
    Six little rosebuds there must be.

[Kate hesitates a moment, as if thinking whether or not she had better come. Then she walks over to the five and they join hands, and circle about her.]

KATE:— Six little rosebuds and what do you think,
    They've sunshine for food, and dew to drink.
    Six little rosebuds fresh and fair
    Smile and nod in the summer air.

[The five stop circling and repeat with Kate, in concert]:—

    Six little girls are we, are we,
    All as quiet as can be,
    Except when we laugh, or play, or sing,
    Or dance about in a rosebud ring.

THE STARS AND STRIPES.

[This exercise is for all of the pupils in the room. Each child should have a small flag in the right hand. All recite in concert, slowly waving the flags back and forth as they remain seated at their desks.]

> The stars and stripes a hundred years
> Have floated towards the sky.
> We will be proud of our country's flag,
> And love it till we die.

First little girl, rising, says:—

> From city homes and country homes,
> From mountain and from plain,
> We hear the echoes of our praise
> And praise our flag again.

All in concert, waving flags:—

> The stars and stripes a hundred years
> Have floated towards the sky;
> We will be proud of our country's flag,
> And love it till we die.

Second little girl, rising:—

> Our country is the fairest land
> On which the sun shines down;
> Our flag is loved three thousand miles,
> In country and in town.

All in concert:—

> The stars and stripes a hundred years
> Have floated towards the sky;
> We will be proud of our country's flag,
> And love it till we die.

First little boy, rising:—

> The people who have loved this flag
> Are living far and near;
> To sixty million faithful hearts
> This flag is very dear.

All in concert:—

> The stars and stripes a hundred years
> Have floated towards the sky;
> We will be proud of our country's flag,
> And love it till we die.

Second little boy, rising:—

> And when we boys in future years
> To be brave men shall grow,
> We will defend our country's flag
> From every foreign foe.

All rise, and standing, wave their flags, and repeat:—

> The stars and stripes a hundred years
> Have floated towards the sky;
> We will be proud of our country's flag,
> And love it till we die.

MINNA C. SMITH.

A FRUIT PIECE.

[FOR FIVE BOYS.]

———

FRANK:— This is an orange, and all the year round
On the trees in Florida they are found;
And sweet white blossoms one always sees
While the green and ripe oranges hang on the trees.

Sometimes they are green when sent away,
But they ripen well before many a day:
Then we may buy them, all yellow and sweet,
And there's nothing *I* like so well to eat.

GEORGE:— This is an apple, so round and red;
They grow in a great many states, 'tis said;
And nothing is prettier for one to see
Than the pink-and-white buds of an apple tree.

Some apples are sour and some are sweet;
And there's nothing *I* like so well to eat.

JAMES:— This is a banana, and from many miles
It comes to us from the southern isles.
It is always warm where bananas grow,
And there's nothing *I* like so well, you know.

HENRY:— Lemons grow in warm countries, too,
If we had no lemons, what should we do?
We make lemonade and it's good, I think;
There's nothing *I* like so well to drink.

CHARLIE:— These are grapes, so purple and sweet;
There's nothing I like so well to eat.
The grapes are dried for raisins too,
And I like them very much, don't you?

COMING MEN.

[FOR TWO BOYS.]

JOHN:—We are the coming men!
  Look at us well, and when
  We shall make the laws for you
  With our judgment proven true,
  You will then look back and say,
  "I knew they would on exhibition day."

  To be strong and to be true
  Is my plan;
  Yonder boy may be a dude
  If he can.
  I prefer the older style,
  Now forgotten for a while,
  Of a man.

  Never mind my hat and coat,
  Prohibition gets my vote;
  And my word shall be my note,—
  That's *my* plan.

CLARENCE [with gesture towards John]:
  He refers to me as a "dude."
  I should scarcely dare be rude
  With his future or his plan.
  I've no doubt he'll be a man,

  But he'll never know the style,
  And the girls will always smile
  When they see his coarse shoe leather,
  Made by the yard for stormy weather.

  "Never mind my coat," says he,
  But ladies *do*. Just look at me,
  My coat fits me—quite the thing—

L *of* C.

Approbation sure to bring.
I will help him laws to make
And fine foreign customs take.

[The two join hands and say together]:

And we both will win success;
We'll deserve it; nothing less.

BESSIE'S GRANDMOTHERS.

[FOR THREE LITTLE GIRLS.]

--

[Grandmamma Gray in cap and spectacles, with knitting work.

Grandmamma White, in similar dress, reading from a book.

Bessie, a small girl, playing with her doll. She puts it down on a chair, and comes and leans against Grandmamma Gray.]

BESSIE:— Tell me a story, Grandmamma,
    I'm tired of my doll and play;
    What did you use to do yourself
    When you were little, all day?

GRANDMAMMA GRAY:—

    When *I* was a little girl, my dear,
    I used to work, not play;
    It would have been thought very queer
    To idle the hours away.

    When *I* was a little girl, my dear,
    I never dreamed of a doll
    Like yours,—of wax! My doll was of rags,
    And she had no hair at all.

BESSIE:—   How funny, how funny, grandmamma!
    Did you love your bald dolly, say?
    Or didn't you and she
      Ever have *any* time to play?

[Grandmamma White puts down her book on her lap,
and listens to the conversation.]

GRANDMAMMA GRAY:—
    No, I used to work most of the time,
      When I was as big as you;
    I made my aprons, pieced a quilt,
      And learned to bake and brew.

    I said "Yes, madam," and "No sir,"
      With most respectful bow;
    It was the proper thing to do;
      Why don't they do so now?

    What do you think, good Mrs. White?
      Wasn't it so in your day?
    And don't you think our olden style,
      Was much the better way?

    I really feel these later ways
      Are not the proper thing,
    These teaching children dancing steps,
      And how to speak and sing.

GRANDMAMMA WHITE:—
    I think it's a pretty custom
      For little ones to grow
    In every grace of head and **heart**,
      And *every* good to know.

    Now, here's our little Bessie,
      I'm sure, dear Grandma Gray,
    She's learned as many useful things
      As we did in our day.

She can sew and darn quite neatly,
  And is respectful quite,
And studies her arithmetic,
  And does her knitting right.

She's learned some pretty verses;
  Bessie, won't you repeat
That Robin poem, darling?
  I think it's very sweet.

BESSIE [stands up, bows to each old lady]:

"In June, in June," sang the robin,
  I will build me a nest so high
In the elm-tree's nodding branches,
  Where harm cannot come nigh.

"I will joy in the earth's glad morning,
  And be glad in the sunshine bright,
I will leave the day no sorrow,
  But sing for its gift of light.

"I will fill the world with sweetness,
  As I build my nest so high
In the elm-tree's nodding branches,
  That reach out towards the sky."

So the nest was built securely,
  And three little robins grew
In safety among the branches
  Under the skies so blue.
                    [Bows and sits down.]

GRANDMAMMA GRAY:—
  That's very pretty, Bessie;
    Perhaps, dear Grandma White,
  There's something in these modern ways
    That I can praise aright.

It's good to work, but it's also good
    To learn the love of beauty;
And children may learn in many ways
    The loveliness of duty.

MAY AND JUNE.

[FOR THREE LITTLE GIRLS.]

CARRIE:— 'T is the time when flowers bloom,
    And the breezes seem to say,
As they drift into the room,
    "Summer's here! Be gay, be gay."

From the roses in the hedge,
    From the grasses bending low,
All things have a joy in June,
    And its beauty all things know.

ADA:— Yes, but all the spring was fair,
Violets blossomed everywhere,
Violets white and violets blue,—
Oh, I love the springtime, too.

All the birds sang everywhere,
And, although the June time's fair,
Something comes in with the spring
That the summer does not bring.

FANNY:— Yes, you both are in the right;
Spring and summer both are bright;
And what makes spring dear to you
Is the promise June proves true.

There's a something in the air,
Saying, " All things bright and fair
Swift are coming. Life's in tune
With the promises of June."

A BUNCH OF PANSIES.

[For four girls and two boys. One of the girls must be
taller and older and one must be younger and smaller
than the other two girls and the little boys.]

ELLA[the tallest girl, standing a little apart from the
other children, who are in a group together]:—

Pansies are for thoughts, they say,
Pansies serious and gay,
Pansies purple, brown, and white,
Pansies dull and pansies bright;
Pansies yellow, pansies blue;
Let them speak their thoughts to you.

WILLIE:— I wear the royal purple;
Kings love my color grand.
I bring you thoughts of splendor
From many a far-off land.

Purple in shadows, morn and eve,
The distant mountains seem;
And there are royal purple lights
When sunset's glories gleam.

GRACE:— Sunshine is yellow, so is gold,
And pansies who this color hold
Lift smiling faces to the sun,
And wear his colors every one.

And if the day is bright or dark,
It does not change their grace;
Each yellow pansy always shows
A sweet and happy face.

MAY:— I'm not so gay as my two friends,
But I am not cast down;
For I know some people like to see
A modest dress of brown.

HERBERT:—A merry blue sailor pansy am I,
I give you thoughts of the sea and sky;
My jacket and cap are finer far
Than those of any jolly jack tar.

BETH [a tiny little girl in a white dress]:—

Let other pansies shine and glow;
I'm but a little thing, I know.
A tiny pansy, dressed in white,
With golden lines on my forehead bright.

I don't suppose you think, at all,
When you look at me, for I'm so small.
I don't bring thought, I'm only meant
To bring you love, and I'm content.

OLD TIMES AND NEW.

[FOR A GIRL AND TWO BOYS.]

FRANK:— I have heard my grandpa say
That it was the old-time way,
Years ago,
To learn a graceful bow,—
Not the stiff ones they teach now,
As you know.

Then boys were always told
To be courteous to the old,
  Come what might,
And to walk with slower pace,
Wear a kindly, smiling face,
  And do right.

CHARLES:— Yet our grandpapas must see
That we'ere always taught to be
  Courteous quite;
If with less of grace I bow,
It's because I don't know how,--
  Honor bright!

When my grandfather was young,
Did he always twist his tongue
  To speak well?
Did he never in his life
Tear his coat or lose his knife?
  He won't tell.

EDITH:— Yes; I've heard my grandma say
That she thinks the old-time way
  Was more wise.
I'm sure I don't know why nor how,
These are good days we have now
  In *my* eyes.

Let us each an effort make,
For our dear grand-parents' sake,
  To succeed;
And to show them if we try
We'll do better by and by,
  Word and deed.

WHAT IS CHRISTMAS?

———

1ST VOICE:—What is Christmas, anyway?
    Why should bells so joyous ring?
    Why should children be so gay,
    And with happy voices sing?

2D VOICE:—Long ago across the sea,
    Christ was born on Christmas day;
    O'er the hills of Galilee
    Shone a star of brightest ray.

    And a mighty angel band
    Sang the joyous song of heaven,
    "Peace, good will, O every land,
    Unto you a child is given."

1ST VOICE:—Why should Christ become a child,
    In this world of pain and woe?
    Why upon that Christmas wild
    Did he come to us below?

2D VOICE:—We were lost in sin and shame
    When our Lord from heaven came down;
    'Twas to save us that He came,
    'Twas to gain for us a crown.

UNISON:—   Wondrous Child of long ago
    Make our youthful hearts as Thine,
    Keep us spotless as the snow,
    Joyous as Thy glad birthtime.

And on merry Christmas days,
    While our hearts with joy are wild,
Let us not forget to praise
    Him who once became a child.

www.ingramcontent.com/pod-product-compliance
Lightning Source LLC
Chambersburg PA
CBHW022342020726
47500CB00004B/1240